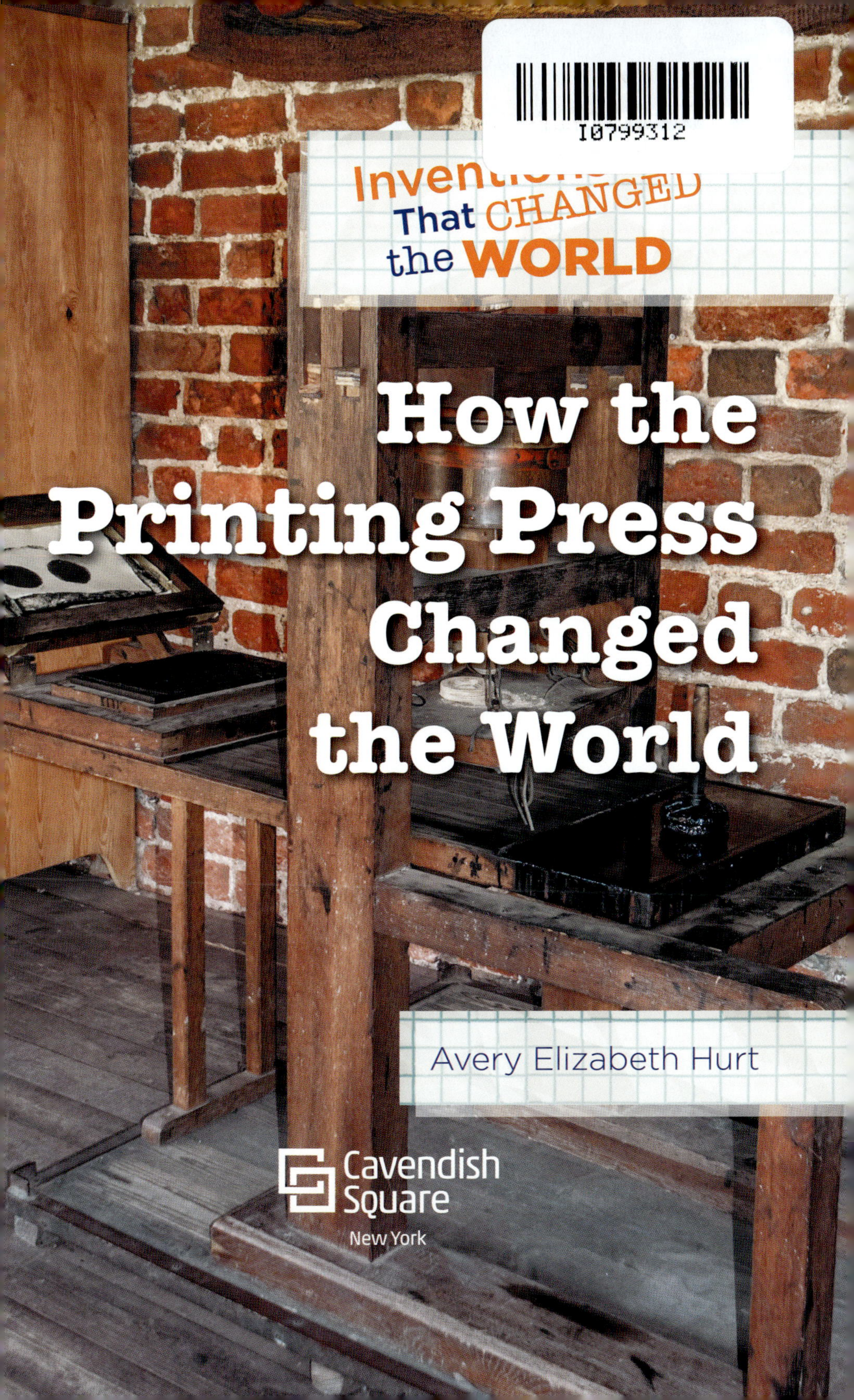

Inventions That CHANGED the WORLD

How the Printing Press Changed the World

Avery Elizabeth Hurt

Cavendish Square
New York

Published in 2019 by Cavendish Square Publishing, LLC
243 5th Avenue, Suite 136, New York, NY 10016

First Edition

Website: cavendishsq.com

Cataloging-in-Publication Data

Names: Hurt, Avery Elizabeth
Title: How the printing press changed the world / Avery Elizabeth Hurt.
Description: New York : Cavendish Square, 2019. |
Series: Inventions that changed the world | Includes glossary and index.
Identifiers: ISBN 9781502641137 (pbk.) | ISBN 9781502641144 (library bound) |
ISBN 9781502641151 (ebook)
Subjects: LCSH: Printing presses--History--Juvenile literature. |
Printing--History--Juvenile literature. | Inventions--Juvenile literature.
Classification: LCC Z124.H87 2019 | DDC 686.2--dc23

Editorial Director: David McNamara
Editor: Kristen Susienka
Copy Editor: Alex Tessman
Associate Art Director: Alan Sliwinski
Designer: Joe Parenteau
Production Coordinator: Karol Szymczuk
Photo Research: J8 Media

The photographs in this book are used by permission and through the courtesy of: Cover Hans Winke/Alamy Stock Photo; p. 4 James Kirkikis/Shutterstock.com; p. 6 Alexey Rotanov/Shutterstock.com; p. 8 Jakub Zak/Shutterstock.com; p. 9 Hulton Archive/Getty Images; p. 11 Universal History Archive/UIG/Getty Images; p. 12 Roger Viollet/Getty Images; p. 14 Fedor Selivanov/Shutterstock.com; p. 15 Steve Estvanik/Shutterstock.com; p. 16 Fine Art Images/Heritage Images/Getty Images; p. 19 Martin33/Shutterstock.com; p. 24 Elitravo/Shutterstock.com; p. 27 North Wind Picture Archives; p. 29 China Photos/Getty Images; p. 31 Imagno/Getty Images; p. 32 Spr/Shutterstock.com; p. 33 SSPL/Getty Images; p. 38 Lukasz Janyst/Shutterstock.com; p. 40 Falkenstein HeinzDieter/Alamy Stock Photo; p. 42 Bob Thomas/Popperfoto/Getty Images; p. 44 Connel/Shutterstock.com; p. 47 FPG/Getty Images; p. 48 Mandel Ngan/AFP/Getty Images; p. 49 Dvortygirl/Wikimedia Commons/File:On demand book printer 1.jpg/CC BY SA 4.0; p. 51 Brad Barket/Getty Images; p. 55 PhotoStock10/Shutterstock.com.

Printed in the United States of America

CONTENTS

This Gutenberg Bible is on display at Yale University.

CHAPTER ONE

When Books Were Rare

A little less than six hundred years ago, in a small city in Germany, something extraordinary happened. Not that many people paid much attention at the time, and those who did didn't realize just how extraordinary it was. A man named Johannes Gutenberg built a machine and used it to print a few copies of the Bible. That was just the beginning. Within a few decades of this remarkable event, the world would be fundamentally different.

Books

Today, more than two million books are published somewhere in the world each year. You can go online to Amazon.com, the world's largest book retailer, and choose from millions of titles. Despite the dominance of Amazon, there are still many brick-and-mortar bookshops. In fact, in recent years, independent bookshops have been thriving, selling books and providing value to local communities.

Books are also available for people who can't afford to buy them. There are over one hundred thousand libraries in the United States alone. Of these, almost ten thousand are available to the public for free. The United States Library of Congress is the largest library in the world. It is home to roughly forty million books and other printed material. The Library of Congress has books and other reading material in more than 450 languages. Schools and universities, cities and towns, and many special interest organizations also have libraries that make books available to people who need or want to read them.

Newspapers and magazines are everywhere too. You can find them in libraries, bookshops, and newsstands. You can also find them online. If you want to read the

The Thomas Jefferson Building, opened in 1897, is the oldest of the three buildings that house the US Library of Congress.

CHECK IT OUT

Libraries existed before the printing press. Monasteries and universities kept precious copies of handwritten works. However, public lending libraries did not come along until much later. The first public lending library that was not associated with a church or university was established in 1598 in Lincolnshire, England. That library, like most public libraries today, was supported by taxes. Though we don't often think about it, libraries are extremely important. In Johannes Gutenberg's time, only the rich could afford books.

Books are much less expensive today, but even now few people outside the very rich could take full advantage of the many works in print without the aid of libraries. In addition to books, libraries offer newspapers, magazines, scholarly journals, and access to the internet. And libraries are staffed with professionals who can help people find what they need.

Without the printing press, there would be no public libraries. Without public libraries, the benefits of the printing press would be available to far fewer people.

Today there are many ways to stay informed. This young man can access and read a variety of newspapers, periodicals, and other informational sources just by tapping his tablet computer.

latest news, you only have to pull out your phone and sign in to your favorite news app, or just browse the web.

Books and other reading material are so much a part of our world, we rarely even think about how astonishing it is that we have them. We usually take for granted this wealth of reading material and easy access to information. But the fact that we have all these books and newspapers—and the freedom to read them—is one of those miracles of history. It never could have happened without Gutenberg's printing press.

When Books Were Rare

Until the middle of the fifteenth century, things had been tough for much of human history. In medieval Europe, usually only members of the clergy and the upper classes could read. People had almost no say about who their leaders were and the decisions those leaders made. There was no real science as we know it today. Superstition and tradition guided people's decisions and beliefs about the world.

Then in the 1400s, a man named Johannes Gutenberg invented a machine that used moveable type to put images of words and letters onto paper. It was not the first time someone had used moveable type to print books. However, Gutenberg made it possible to print faster and more efficiently. Once his press was in action, books could be made in hours rather than months.

At first the world-rocking effects of the new machine were not obvious. Bibles and other books could be printed much more quickly now, but still most people couldn't read anyway. The Roman Catholic Church had a tight grip on society. For people living in Europe at the time,

This illustration from a fourteenth-century manuscript shows children studying their schoolbooks. However, at that time, very few children were fortunate enough to be able to study books.

it was all but unimaginable that anything would change. Yet it did. Ordinary people learned to read. The more they read, the more they thought critically about their world. They began to share their ideas with others—a much easier task now that they could have these ideas printed. Together they came up with different and better ways to organize society. They took a close look at the natural world and shared their discoveries. They learned to think for themselves. They started changing the world.

DID YOU KNOW:

Some scholars estimate that before Gutenberg there were only thirty thousand books in all of Europe.

Less than seventy years after Gutenberg printed his first Bible, the Catholic Church was split in two by the Protestant Reformation. Within another half a century, science was beginning to bloom. By the eighteenth century, citizens were questioning the right of their leaders to rule and demanding a say in their governments. All of these changes and many more were made possible by a technology that gave people the ability to print books quickly and easily.

Effects of the Printing Press Today

We are still feeling the effects of the huge changes the printing press brought to the world. Today, roughly

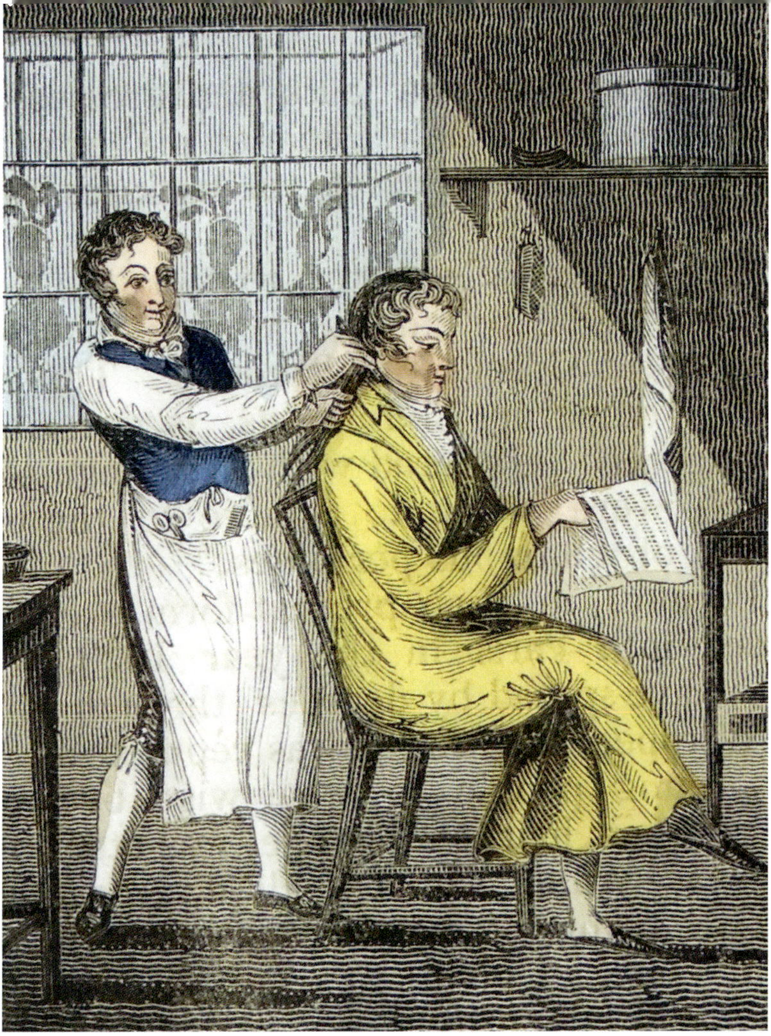

This illustration from 1821 shows a man reading a newspaper while getting a haircut. Without the printing press, gaining such easy access to news would not have been possible.

90 percent of the people in the world are literate. The majority of the world's people live in countries where the people have at least some voice in their governments. Science influences many global decisions. However, the way we make books and share reading material is still changing. The revolution that Johannes Gutenberg started in a small city in Germany almost six hundred years ago is still changing the world.

This illustration shows Johannes Gutenberg, circa 1395–1468.

CHAPTER TWO

The Man from Mainz and His Mysterious Machine

The printing press was a remarkable invention. However, without another big invention, it would not have been needed.

First There Was Writing

About five thousand years ago, in three different places in the world—China, the near East, and Mesoamerica—people figured out how to turn words and sounds into symbols. These symbols could then be carved on stone, scratched into wet clay, or eventually drawn on paper. At first people used this method of communication mostly for bookkeeping. In fact, one of the oldest existing examples of writing is a receipt for the sale of farm animals. However, it wasn't long before people began writing down their laws, their history, their stories and poems.

This ancient stone was carved with cuneiform, one of the earliest kinds of writing. Cuneiform was developed by the Sumerians, an early Mesopotamian culture that developed in what is today southern Iraq.

People in ancient Egypt used a plant called papyrus to make a flat surface, somewhat like paper, to write on. The English word "paper" comes from the word papyrus (as do the words for paper in most European languages). In places where papyrus didn't grow, people often wrote on animal skins that were stretched very thin. This was called parchment. If it was very high quality and made from calfskin, it was called vellum.

In ancient China, people carved words onto bones and tortoise shells. About two thousand years ago, the Chinese invented paper. Paper was much smoother and easier to write on than papyrus or parchment. It was also much cheaper. The Arab world began using paper not long after the Chinese invented it. However, paper didn't become popular in Europe until the twelfth century.

No matter what material they were writing on, once people figured out how to get their words on paper, they began making books. Sometimes a "book" was actually a scroll, a long piece of papyrus or parchment that could be rolled up for storage. In medieval Europe, books were divided into separate pages that were then sewn together. Wooden covers were placed on the outside of books to protect the pages. A book made like this is called a codex. (The word "codex" comes from a Latin word that means "tree trunk" or "block of wood." The plural form is "codices.")

People took great care to use beautiful handwriting and lovely illustrations, or illumination, in their books. Many of them were like works of art. Books of any kind were very rare and expensive, though. Books had to be

This illuminated manuscript from the medieval period in Europe is a lovely example of the detailed artwork in these beautiful and expensive handmade books.

This painting depicts St. Jerome working in a medieval scriptorium, or writing room. It was painted around 1485 by an artist in the Monasterio de Santa María del Parral near Segovia, Spain.

handmade and hand copied one at a time. Making each copy of a book took a great deal of time and effort. The books were often very beautiful and always valuable.

Books were copied by scribes. A scribe was a professional who was trained in writing. In addition to copying books, scribes wrote letters, copied legal documents, and took care of other correspondence for people who could not read and write—and few people could in those days. Oddly, not all of the people who copied books were trained scribes. Some copyists, as they were called, were not literate. They couldn't read the book they were copying. They simply drew what they saw on the page. Even when scribes knew how to read and write, they might not be able to read the language they were copying in. Many medieval monks could read Latin but not Greek.

Scribes didn't just copy the Bible. They also copied and preserved Greek and Latin mythological and literacy texts. However, as the Christian religion grew and spread in Europe after the sixth century or so, these works were neglected in favor of religious works. Most scribes were monks, and monasteries typically had libraries. They also had rooms called "scriptoria." This was where scribes would make copies of the Bible, religious works, and other important texts for their libraries.

Tedious Work

Being a scribe was a valuable position in a medieval monastery. The work they did was important and took a great deal of skill. Some scribes were allowed to skip their daily prayers so they would have more time to work. Scribes did not have to do other jobs, such as work in the garden or the kitchen, but scribing wasn't easy work. Copying a book was a tedious process. It could take months to complete a book. It took time to write everything out by hand. Other things made the process tedious and time consuming as well. Medieval scribes wrote with goose quill pens that had to be hand carved, hand sharpened, and frequently dipped in ink. The ink had to be made by hand too. If a scribe made a mistake, he had to carefully scrape the ink off the parchment and begin again. Most medieval scribes toiled on their manuscripts for at least six hours a day, sometimes longer. And they didn't have nice workstations with comfortable office chairs.

Under these circumstances, scribes often made mistakes. Some mistakes were small, but even a small mistake would be repeated when that book itself was copied, so the mistakes multiplied as books were copied. The original version of a book might be lost or unavailable, so it would be difficult if not impossible for a reader to find out exactly what the writer had meant. In any case, monks were not allowed to correct mistakes they found in the books they were copying; they had to copy them exactly as they found them.

One common error when copying material by hand is called the eye-skip. This is when the scribe's eye jumped from a word he was reading to the next instance of the same word. That may be later in the same line or further down the page, but either way, some of the text was missed. If the scribe's eye skipped back to a previous instance of a word, he might accidentally repeat a section of the text he had already copied. Mistakes like these were frustrating, especially when the text being copied was very important. When texts had to be copied by hand at great expense, only important texts were copied.

Copying texts was hard work. In the margins of one medieval codex, a scribe wrote, "Thank, God, it will soon be dark." Most scribes were probably happy when sunset arrived and they could stop for the day. However, it's

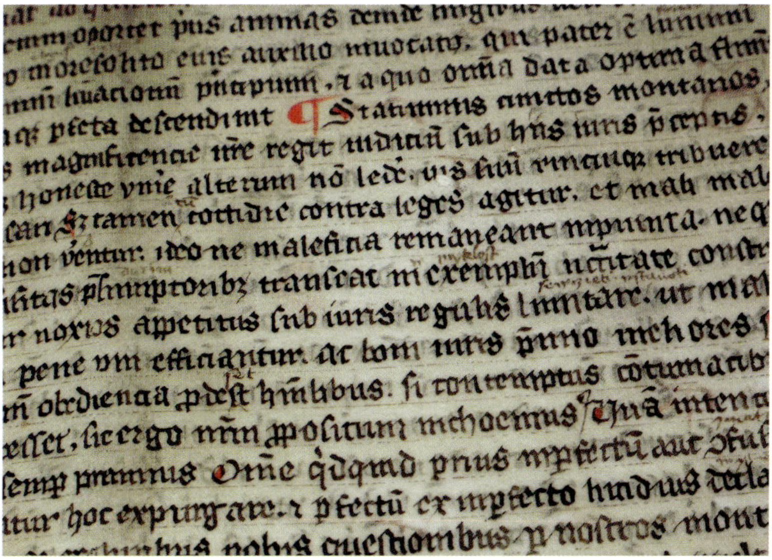

This close-up of the text of a medieval manuscript shows the kinds of scripts scribes copied. Reproducing these letters was very much like drawing or painting.

doubtful that they considered the process drudgery. For many scribes the work was a craft, perhaps even an art. Reproducing the handwritten letters and the beautiful illustrations was a way to show devotion to God and also to add beauty to the world.

The Church

During the Middle Ages in Western Europe, the Roman Catholic Church increased its wealth and power enormously. The Church, as it was called, taught that Jesus Christ had established the Catholic Church to see that everyone was able to take advantage of his grace and salvation. The only way to Jesus, and therefore salvation, was through the Church. The life of a medieval person

STILL MAKING ERRORS

The invention of the printing press eliminated the many mistakes made by scribes copying works by hand. However, it did not eliminate all mistakes. Many of the early printed Bibles had mistakes too. Some of them were funny. One reads, "pay for peace" instead of, "pray for peace." In a Bible printed in 1807, the phrase "who hath ears to hear" was mistakenly printed as "who has ears to ears." That edition has come to be known as the "Ears to Ears Bible." A Bible printed in the 1600s leaves out the word "no" in a crucial spot. Psalm 14:1 says, "The fool says in his heart, 'There is a God.'" Oops. That should have been the fool says there is no God. One mistake, by replacing the word "princes," seems to be commenting on all these mistakes. A 1702 Bible has King David saying, "Printers have persecuted me without a cause."

was encompassed by the Church. Births, marriages, and deaths were all rituals based on Church teachings.

The Church and rulers were closely linked as well. Kings, queens, and even local leaders were expected to support the Church and follow and enforce its rules. At this time, it was believed that God put kings in charge of their countries and ruled through them. As long as the people believed this, kings had complete authority over the societies they ruled, and that rule was justified by religion. To protest the decision of a king would be to protest against God. To overthrow a king would be to go against the will of God. This helped rulers keep their power. However, this also put kings at the mercy of the Church. As long as rulers derived their authority from the Church, they would not be wise to challenge any of the Church's teachings. So, in fact, the Church had as much if not more power than kings and other rulers.

The Church also had considerable economic power. People were required to give one-tenth of their earnings to the Church. Sometimes the Church also made money by charging for various services, such as baptisms and weddings. The Church also owned a great deal of land, which they could rent out to famers for profit. Scholars estimate that by the time Gutenberg built his press, the Church owned one-third of all the land in Europe.

Most people in medieval Europe were devoted to the teachings of the Church—or at least pretended to be—and the Church worked very hard to keep it that way. Heretics, people who dared to disagree with the teachings of the Church, were punished, often severely.

Most universities at that time were supported by the Church as well. Now, add to this the fact that books were expensive and literacy was rare, and you have a situation in which the Church controls not only politics but almost all learning. The Church told people what to believe and controlled a great deal of how they lived their lives. The Church was so much a part of medieval life that few people ever thought to question its authority. By the end of the medieval period, however, this would change radically, thanks to Gutenberg and his printing press.

Magic Mirrors and Mysterious Machines

Johannes Gutenberg was born in Mainz, Germany, sometime around 1395. Mainz was typical of late-medieval cities in many ways. The unpaved streets were often filled with mud, and sewage ran in open ditches along the sides of the streets. Over the years, many of the city's inhabitants had died during periodic outbreaks of plague. By the time Gutenberg began building his press, the town was home to around six thousand people—and forty churches.

Though Mainz was not large, it was important. The archbishop there was one of the men, called "electors," who chose the kings of Germany. However, the city was not entirely controlled by the Church. Old wealthy families, called patricians, and an up-and-coming middle class of artisans, such as masons and goldsmiths, had a great deal of say in local politics. However, the two groups did not get along.

The city had a peculiar financial arrangement. Wealthy citizens who could afford to would occasionally loan the city money. The families would then be paid interest, called annuities, on these loans *forever.* After the citizens who made the loans died, payments would continue to be paid to their heirs. The city's artisans were heavily taxed in order to make these outrageous payments to the city's patricians. The artisans organized themselves into guilds and competed with the patricians for political power.

Gutenberg came from a patrician family. During a period when the guilds had gained some political power, his family's annuities were cut in half. About this time, Gutenberg left Mainz and moved to Strasbourg, then a part of Germany. Strasbourg was a much larger city of around twenty-five thousand people. There he seems to have decided to develop some skills of his own. In Strasbourg, he set up a workshop and tried his hand at several enterprises, including developing a technique for polishing gemstones. He became a goldsmith and developed some skill at metalwork and jewelry making.

Strasbourg was home to Aachen Cathedral, which housed religious relics. There people could view the robe Mary wore on the night Jesus was born, the swaddling clothes of the baby Jesus, and the cloth Jesus wore on the cross. Every seven years, pilgrims would make the journey to Strasbourg to see these holy relics. Pilgrims to Aachen would hold small hand mirrors up to these holy fabrics. They believed that the mirrors would store blessings from the relics. Then later when they were back home, they could look in the mirrors and receive the blessings again.

In Gutenberg's time, Strasbourg was a part of the German empire. Now it is in the Alsace region of France. Close to the border between France and Germany, Strasbourg today has elements of both cultures.

Though pilgrimages were serious spiritual matters, they were also fun outings for the pilgrims. Pilgrims often bought souvenirs and special tokens of their journey to take back home with them.

By this time, Gutenberg knew not only how to make mirrors but how to frame them in beautiful metalwork. The pilgrimage was a great business opportunity for the ambitious young man. He would make mirrors and sell them to the pilgrims when they descended on Strasbourg for the 1439 pilgrimage.

Gutenberg persuaded some wealthy men in Strasbourg to invest in his scheme. Things didn't go as planned, however. That year's pilgrimage was canceled because of another outbreak of plague. Gutenberg and his investors had a legal dispute about what should be done with the materials they had planned to use to make the mirrors. The records of the court case that followed hint that the group was working on some kind of valuable and mysterious "press." Gutenberg settled with his investors, but as a part of the settlement, he asked that some *formen*—"forms" in English—be melted down to keep them from falling into the wrong hands. It is not at all clear from the court records what these were. There is no record of Gutenberg again until four years later, when he returned to Mainz.

A New Scheme

Now settled back in his hometown, Gutenberg began a new project—this one much bigger than pilgrim mirrors. In 1450, he borrowed eight hundred guilders (Germany's currency at that time) at 6 percent interest from a man named Johann Fust. This was an enormous amount of money and a considerable amount of interest. Fust was a wealthy Mainz guild officer and was well connected in the Mainz business world. We don't know how much Gutenberg told Fust about his plans, but he must have convinced the moneylender he was onto something big, because Fust himself had to borrow some of the money he loaned to Gutenberg.

DID YOU KNOW:

Fust's name is sometimes spelled "Faust." This caused some to speculate that the fictional character Dr. Faustus, who traded his soul to the devil for knowledge, was based on Gutenberg's financial backer.

Gutenberg spent the money outfitting a new shop. However, he failed to make the interest payments on the loan. Again, it looks as if Fust had a great deal of faith in Gutenberg's idea, because he nonetheless loaned Gutenberg another eight hundred guilders! This loan, however, came with a condition. Fust required that Gutenberg hire Peter Schöffer as an apprentice in his shop. Schöffer was a family connection of Fust's (and would later marry Fust's daughter). Before he came to work for Gutenberg, Schöffer, though still young, was a highly trained scribe, engraver, and calligrapher working in Paris. It is not entirely clear why Fust was so eager for Gutenberg to take the young man on as an apprentice. If Gutenberg had any reservations, history does not record them. In any case, Schöffer was well qualified, and Gutenberg desperately needed more money for his project.

The project, of course, was a printing press. Apparently the mysterious machine mentioned in the lawsuit between Gutenberg and his partners back in Strasbourg was a precursor of the printing press Gutenberg eventually built in Mainz. No wonder he was so eager to keep his trade secrets!

With money in hand, Gutenberg got busy. By 1451, he was producing books. He began with rather small projects. He printed a Latin primer, or textbook, called *Ars Minor*, a poem, and a few other small things. These smaller works gave him a chance to get the kinks out of his new printing system. Eventually, though, he was ready for a much more ambitious project. In 1455, he printed the full text of the Vulgate, the most common

This is a hand-colored woodcut of Gutenberg's first printing press. Note the screw press, the large platen, and the Bibles on the floor around it. In reality, the precious books would not have been placed so casually.

Latin translation of the Bible. He included all the beautiful artwork as well. Copies of it exist still today, and it is a gorgeous book. It is likely that Schöffer, being a former scribe, had something to do with the decision to print Bibles. He must have been invaluable when it came to preparing the artwork for the books.

Gutenberg almost certainly developed his printing press as a way to make money. It would eventually be a very profitable machine indeed. Unfortunately, Gutenberg himself did not see much of the profit. He did, however, get the credit for it. He went down in history as the man who invented printing. As we shall see, that is something of an exaggeration. It is no exaggeration, however, to say that Gutenberg's invention changed the world.

A Chinese artisan demonstrates Chinese block printing.

CHAPTER THREE

The Changes Begin

Gutenberg's machine was an amazing device. However, it was not the first printing press ever made. Printing had been around for a long time. Nevertheless, there is no question that it had a bigger impact than any printing methods that came before it.

Who Got There First?

As early as 700 CE, the Chinese were using block printing. They would draw a picture on a block of wood then carve out everything except the parts they wanted in the final print. Then they would coat with ink the part of the wood that had not been carved away and press it onto paper, making a print. They did something similar using clay tiles. One of the oldest surviving books printed by this method is *The Diamond Sutra*, a classic Buddhist text. The 17.5-foot (5.3-meter) scroll was printed in 868 CE.

Block printing allowed people to make many prints of the same page, but it was still very slow and tedious because every page had to be carved separately. If you had a twenty-page book, you needed to carve twenty blocks or tiles. The answer to this problem was moveable type.

Gutenberg's press used moveable type. Because of this, he is often said to have invented the technique. However, the Chinese got to this first too. Four hundred years before Gutenberg was born, a Chinese blacksmith named Bi Sheng carved individual characters (rather than entire pages of a book) into very thin pieces of clay. He fired the clay to harden the pieces. When he wanted to print a page of text, he arranged the pieces in a metal frame. The clay tiles could be mixed and matched in any number of ways. Then he would ink the characters and press them into paper, just as you would do with block printing, but without having to carve each page. Over the years, other Chinese printers refined the method of moveable type printing. Moveable type was used in other parts of Asia as well. In 1377, a Buddhist monk in Korea used metal moveable type to print a collection of Buddhist sayings.

Solving the Big Problems

So if Gutenberg didn't invent printing and didn't invent moveable type, then why is he such a big deal? Well, for one thing he did invent a printing press that mechanized the printing of books. To make that work, he had to solve a few problems along the way. In order to make a moveable

Printing elaborately designed and illustrated—illuminated—manuscripts, such as this codex from a Benedictine monastery in Austria, required thicker inks and sturdier paper than that used in hand copying.

type that worked well enough to support mass printing of books and other literature, he had to come up with a type of ink that worked better than calligraphy ink, a way to cast the metal type he would use to print the letters, and a machine to make it all happen rapidly and efficiently. If he could not solve these problems, his invention would, like that of Bi Sheng, be lost to history.

The ink used at the time in Germany worked beautifully for the calligraphy that was used to hand copy books. However, it was far too thin and watery for a printing press. It would soak nicely into the sturdy European paper, but would slide right off the printer's metal typefaces. After much experimentation, Gutenberg came up with a thicker, oil-based ink that spread evenly and looked nice and glossy when dry on the page.

In order to solve the problem of the metal type, Gutenberg developed a special alloy—a combination of metals—that would melt at a low temperature. This way it could be poured into wooden molds to make the

Cast metal type was one of the most important features of Gutenberg's press. It has changed many times over the years. Today we have a wide choice of fonts and typefaces.

metal typefaces. However, once cooled, this metal had to be hard enough to stand up to the rigors of repeated use. One of the most important features of Gutenberg's system was that the type could be used again and again. In order to print a new book, you did not have to carve and cast the letters all over again; you just rearranged the ones you already had.

Now that he had those problems solved, he had to come up with a way to press the letters onto the paper. For all his clever solutions to the problem of ink and molds, Gutenberg's press would never have been worth much if it couldn't press evenly and consistently. Gutenberg didn't have to look far for a solution to this problem. Screw presses had been used for centuries to press grapes to make wine or olives to make olive oil. Gutenberg adapted this ancient technology for his needs, so that each page no longer had to be hand pressed. He added a heavy, flat wooden or iron board, called a platen, to the wine press. When the screws were tightened, the platen came down and pressed the paper evenly onto the inked type. This is an area where Gutenberg's invention went far beyond previous printing systems.

Gutenberg's press worked like this. The letters and other characters to be used in a book were carved in wood then cast in metal, called type. The characters for each page would be placed in a metal frame—backwards so

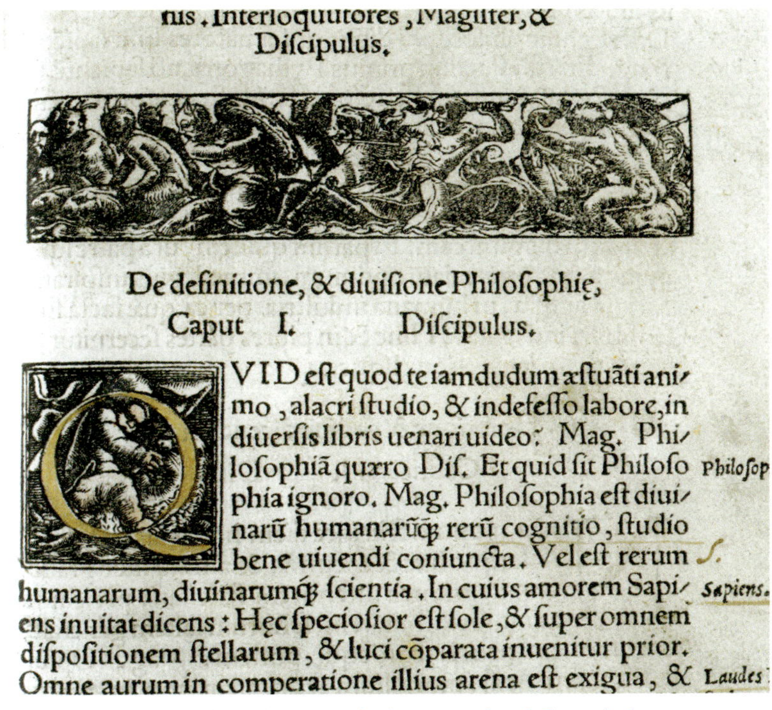

nis . Interloquutores , Magiſter, &
Diſcipulus.

De definitione, & diuiſione Philoſophiȩ,
Caput I. Diſcipulus.

QVID eſt quod te iamdudum æſtuãti animo, alacri ſtudio, & indefeſſo labore, in diuerſis libris uenari uideo? Mag. Philoſophiã quæro. Diſ. Et quid ſit Philoſophia ignoro. Mag. Philoſophia eſt diuinarũ humanarũq; rerũ cognitio, ſtudio bene uiuendi coniuncta. Vel eſt rerum humanarum, diuinarumq; ſcientia. In cuius amorem Sapiens inuitat dicens: Hȩc ſpecioſior eſt ſole, & ſuper omnem diſpoſitionem ſtellarum, & luci cõparata inuenitur prior. Omne aurum in comperatione illius arena eſt exigua, &

Philoſop
Sapiens.
Laudes

This book, an encyclopedia intended as a textbook for scholars, was printed in 1503, not long after Gutenberg's technology began to spread throughout Europe.

that when printed it would come out right. The letters were then covered with ink. A piece of paper (or sometimes parchment) was placed on top of the frame. The press was cranked down to lower the platen onto the paper. This pressed the inked letters against the paper, making a print. Then the pages were hung up to dry. It could be done over and over again until you had as many copies as you needed.

For the first time anywhere, books could be mass-produced. This was the greatest advance in communication since the invention of writing. The consequences would be enormous.

Keeping the Books

Gutenberg was a master at overcoming technological challenges. However, he was not so good at dealing with financial challenges. Though in the long run printing would be a profitable venture, getting the process started was very costly.

Gutenberg was not a man to cut corners. He could have used only the bare minimum of typefaces—uppercase and lowercase letters, punctuation and a few necessary symbols. However, he was not aiming to simply reprint the words in the Bible. He wanted his version to look exactly like the handwritten Latin manuscript that scribes had copied and people were familiar with. Therefore, he manufactured at least 290 different typefaces for his Bible. Each page had almost three thousand characters, and two pages had

CAN'T QUITE MAKE THAT OUT

The style of type Gutenberg's printer used was called Gothic or Blackletter. It looked very much like the handwritten manuscripts he was printing. It was exactly the look Gutenberg wanted, and it made beautiful books. However, it wasn't easy to read.

In Venice, a decade or so after Gutenberg published the Bible, a Frenchman named Nicolas Jenson developed a type with straight lines and a uniform design. Because Jenson's design was based on the engravings on Roman statues, it was called Roman type. It was far easier to read and also cheaper to produce than Gothic type.

Many typefaces have been designed since, but the move from Gothic to Roman was a major innovation in the readability of printed texts. Today the word Roman is used to designate type that is straight. Slanted type is called "italic."

to be set with type at any given time to keep the process going. In the end he needed thousands of bits of cast type just to keep the press running. There was also the matter of artwork. For the first editions, the drawings had to be carved and painted by hand. Of course, like the typefaces, they could be reused, but the initial investment was considerable. In addition, there was the cost of paper, ink, and labor.

Gutenberg was not a good businessperson, but Johann Fust was. While Gutenberg was refining his technique and building his printing press, Fust was very patient about collecting the money Gutenberg owed him. However, once the invention was perfect and the Bibles were rolling off the press, Fust called in the loans. Not surprisingly, Gutenberg was unable to repay his debts. He certainly would have been had he been given more time to sell the Bibles. Fust, however, was unwilling to wait. He took Gutenberg to court. The court sided with Fust and awarded him all of Gutenberg's equipment. Gutenberg's apprentice, Peter Schöffer, had by this time become as much of an artisan of printing as he had once been of calligraphy. He joined with Fust in a new printing company called Fust & Schöffer, which employed many of the workers who had trained with Gutenberg. They produced many more books as beautiful as the Gutenberg Bibles.

Some historians have speculated that Fust planned this all along. He had, some say, pressured Gutenberg to hire Schöffer in order to have a spy in the workshop learning Gutenberg's techniques. His approach does seem suspicious. He insisted on having a close associate in the shop. He even went so far as to borrow money to invest in the venture. Then as soon as he knew it would be profitable, he took everything and started his own printing company. We can never know his motives, of course. There may be much more to this story that is lost to history.

In any case, Fust and Schöffer did not manage to keep the printing technology to themselves for long. City politics intervened once again. In 1462, the pope sent a new archbishop to take charge of the city of Mainz. The current archbishop resisted and closed the city's gates against the newcomer. Forces of the new archbishop scaled the city walls and took over Mainz. They then expelled the citizens who had been loyal to the old archbishop. As a result, the dozen or so men who had worked in Gutenberg's shop and learned his trade scattered out across Europe, taking their new skills with them. In less than two decades, every country in Europe had at least one printing press. By 1500, there were about 240 printing shops on the European continent.

Learning to Read

Gutenberg's Bible was in Latin. At that time, Latin was the primary language of the Catholic Church and of the educated classes. Before the printing press, almost all books were written in Latin. Since so few ordinary people could read, there was little need for books in their local languages. However, once the printing press

This monument to Polish astronomer Nicolaus Copernicus stands today in Torun, Poland.

was invented, this began to change quickly. More and more religious and scholarly books were translated into the languages ordinary people spoke in their countries and towns. New books were being written and published in these languages as well. As more books became available to read, more people learned how. When Gutenberg built his press, probably less than 30 percent of adults in Europe could read—and most of those readers were clergy or members of the ruling classes. After the printing press, literacy began to quickly spread. This was to have an enormous effect on society.

In 1543, Nicolaus Copernicus, a Polish astronomer, published a book called *On the Revolution of Heavenly Spheres*, explaining that Earth revolves around the sun. This was a dangerous thing to say, since it contradicted the Catholic Church's position that Earth was the center of the solar system. But thanks to the printing press, Copernicus's arguments and equations spread quickly. Other scientists were able to build on his work. Many other scientific works were published in the coming years. Today, science depends on scientists being able to read the works of others, and to share their work with a wide range of other scientists in many other places and get feedback from them. That was difficult if not impossible before the printing press. After the printing press, science made huge strides.

By the end of the 1500s, pamphlets and newsletters had begun to appear. This ability to spread whatever ideas one had and get a wide readership for them would challenge the power not only of the Catholic Church, but of civil authorities as well. In the seventeenth and eighteenth centuries, the Enlightenment was enabled by the spread of learning made possible by the printing press. The Enlightenment was a philosophical revolution that valued reason and experimentation above accepting the word of authority. Enlightenment ideas contributed directly to modern science and the founding of the United States and other democratic governments.

Mixed Reviews

In the early days of the print revolution, church leaders seemed to approve. In 1455, when the ink was hardly dry on Gutenberg's first Bible, the man who would eventually become Pope Pius II praised it warmly. He wrote to a friend that, "A marvelous man had been promoting the Bible." The Catholic Church saw the new technology as a useful way to make sure its instructions about ceremonies and liturgy could be shared with local priests without mistakes creeping in. In fact, some of Gutenberg's early printing commissions came from the Catholic Church.

However, it didn't take long for church leaders to realize that the printing press posed a challenge to their

This sketch shows Pope Innocent VIII.

authority. In 1487, Pope Innocent VIII issued a ruling that required printshops to get approval from the Catholic Church for any and all books they printed.

In 1501, Pope Alexander VI doubled down on these restrictions. He stressed that this applied not just to religious works but to works published by universities and private companies as well. Local authorities that did not enforce this rule could be subject to excommunication. If they did enforce it, they would be rewarded with a portion of the considerable fines collected from the printer who defied the law. Censorship by the Catholic Church was nothing new. It had always sought to control books being reproduced. But before the printing press, it had been much easier to prevent the circulation of material it disapproved of. Afterward, it became increasingly difficult and eventually impossible for the Catholic Church to control the flow of knowledge and information.

It turned out that the Church was right to worry.

Ninety-Five Gripes

Martin Luther was a Catholic monk and professor of theology at the University of Wittenberg in Germany. He was a devout man but had some serious problems with certain church practices. He was particularly bothered by the sale of indulgences. These were somewhat like coupons that people could purchase to excuse them from punishment for certain sins. The pope had been selling these to raise money to rebuild St. Peter's Basilica, an important church in Rome. It was, in Luther's view, a terribly corrupt practice. He objected to the idea that salvation could be bought. He said that the pope did not have the authority to pardon people for their sins; only God could do that. He also objected to the Catholic Church's treatment of the poor. Luther wrote out his complaint in a list of ninety-five objections, what came to be called the Ninety-Five Theses. One day in the autumn of 1517, he boldly nailed this heresy to the door of the Church in Wittenberg. (Actually, scholars think that he posted them on something like a bulletin board, asking other scholars to meet and discuss them. But the image of the monk defiantly nailing his criticism to the front door of the church has stuck in the world's imagination.) Luther hoped to spark a debate that would ultimately result in the reform of the Catholic Church. Instead he sparked a debate that would eventually tear it apart.

Had it not been for the printing press, Luther's efforts probably wouldn't have spread further than Wittenberg and may have remained an academic debate. But the new technology allowed his writings to be spread and read by many. It also made it possible for people to read the Bible for themselves and see if they agreed with Luther or the pope.

The Catholic Church convicted Luther of heresy and demanded that he renounce his views. He refused, famously saying, "*Hier stehe ich; ich kann nicht anders.*" (Here I stand; I cannot do otherwise.) A few years earlier this would have been enough to get Luther burned at the stake. However, many of the rulers in Germany at the time were more sympathetic to Luther than to the pope, and they protected him. Luther continued to write pamphlets and essays—in German—critical of the Catholic Church. Thanks to the printing press, many people in Germany and elsewhere in Europe read them. Luther became quite popular. This also made it harder for the Catholic Church to silence him. Eventually, in an event called the Protestant

Martin Luther was a scholar and religious reformer who attempted to reform the Catholic Church, but instead launched the Protestant Reformation.

DID YOU KNOW:

In what may be one of the greatest ironies in history, one of Gutenberg's earliest printing commissions was printing indulgences for the Catholic Church.

Reformation, Luther's followers broke away from the Catholic Church and formed a new branch of Christianity called Protestantism.

By the early 1600s, newspapers began to appear in and around Strasbourg. Much like Bibles had done for the Reformation, newspapers gave ordinary citizens a chance to discuss politics, share their views, and consider the views of others. The free and widely available exchange of ideas made possible by the printing press changed the course of the Christian religion. It also changed the way governments ruled their people. Now that people had learned that they could think for themselves and challenge their rulers, they began to do so. Eventually this would lead to the idea that people should decide who their rulers were. It would lead to the end of the divine right of kings and the growth of democracy.

When the first primer rolled off Gutenberg's printing press, a chain of events began that could not be stopped. These changes didn't stop with the Enlightenment or the Protestant Reformation or the birth of democracy. We are still living with its legacy today.

A world full of books is one of the legacies of Gutenberg's press.

CHAPTER FOUR

Still Making Revolutions

After Gutenberg's breakthrough, printing technology continued to evolve. The revolution sparked by his printing press was one of the first that changed the way the world communicates. However, it was far from the last. The effects of the invention of the printing press are still being felt today.

Innovations and Improvements

Over the years, printers improved the printing press. By the late eighteenth century, printing presses were made out of metal instead of wood. Modifications using gears, levers, weights, and counterweights helped make the printing process easier and more efficient. By the 1800s, steam was used to power presses, further mechanizing printing. In 1844, Richard March Hoe invented the rotary press. This breakthrough technique passed paper between two cylinders, one to support the paper and one to hold the type. The first rotary press could print up to eight thousand copies an hour, making it possible for newspapers to print many copies of each edition. This greatly increased the reach of journalism, so much so that collectively the journalism industry came to be called "the press."

In the early twentieth century, the invention of the offset press revolutionized printing once again. In offset printing, thin, engraved aluminum plates transfer an image not directly to the paper but to a rubber sheet, called a blanket. Then the blanket transfers the image to paper.

The process of setting the type was mechanized as well. Though Gutenberg's method was much faster than hand copying, it was still time consuming. In 1884, Ottmar Mergenthaler of Baltimore, Maryland, gave the world a much faster method. It was called the Linotype machine. The Linotype was a typesetting machine that cast molten lead into lines of type (a "line o' type") rather than individual letters. The printing press had automated the pressing of books. The Linotype machine automated the selection and arrangement of type. One Linotype operator using a keyboard could do the work of ten people arranging the type by hand. These huge, hot, clattering machines were not replaced at the nation's newspapers until the late twentieth century when the desktop computer made its way to the newsroom.

The first Linotype machine, shown here, was installed at the *New York Tribune* in 1886. The machines were used in newspaper offices until the 1980s.

Desktop Publishing

The biggest innovation in printing since Gutenberg was the personal computer. In 1985, a set of software, known collectively as desktop publishing, changed the printing world more than anything since Gutenberg printed his first primer.

These days, computer programs are used to do virtually all the work of publishing. An author writes a book, article, or another piece of text on a word processing program, such as Microsoft Word. Then the computer file is passed on to the designer. The designer uses other computer programs, such as Adobe InDesign and Adobe Photoshop, to arrange the print, illustrations,

The newsroom of the *Washington Post* has many computer workstations. All the writing and design is done on desktop computers, then sent to the print department for printing. The Linotype machine is no longer necessary.

and photographs on the page. No, carving, engraving, or Linotype machine is necessary. An electronic file containing all this information is sent, usually by email, to the printshop. The information is transferred from the computer file to the printing machine for printing.

Just Hit "Send"

Offset printing is still around today. It is excellent for printing thousands of copies of books or magazines. However, it can be expensive to make the plates for each page. Until recently, printing fewer than one thousand copies of a book didn't make financial sense. The price per book would be far too much. If a publishing company couldn't sell at least one thousand copies, it would likely lose money on the book. Print-on-demand

(POD) technology made that problem a thing of the past. With print on demand, books are printed directly from electronic files and not transferred to a printing plate. A single copy of a book can be printed just as easily as one thousand copies. A POD printer works a lot like a large, fancy version of a desktop printer—both systems use either electrically charged toner or ink squirted through tiny holes to make prints. POD technology makes it easier for publishers to keep books available for customers to buy even after sales begin to wane. University publishing houses, which tend to sell far fewer copies of a given title, frequently use POD publishing.

All of these have been innovations and advancements on Gutenberg's basic invention. But these days, you don't even need to print a book or article for people to read

In this print-on-demand book printer, pages are produced in one printer, covers on another, then all are sent to the third machine for binding.

it. Anything you write can be shared with people all around the world without ever being printed. At one time "publishing" a book or newspaper meant spending thousands of dollars on paper, printing equipment, shipping, and storage of the printed books or magazines. Now it can mean buying relatively inexpensive computers and software, and clicking the "publish" or "send" button on a computer screen. Where does that text go when you hit "send"? Just about everywhere, and almost instantaneously.

Gutenberg of the Modern Age

The internet was invented in 1967. By connecting to the internet, any computer can communicate with any other computer also connected to the internet. The internet allows computers to pass information to each other much the same way the post office delivers mail. In this analogy, the internet is not the mail. It is the system of postal trucks that delivers the mail and the network of routes they follow. All sorts of things are sent along postal routes: letters, bills, birthday cards, packages. People put lots of things on the internet too—email, instant messages, phone conversations, music downloads. But in order to send a message over the internet—an email, for example—someone had to write programs for that specific use.

In the mid-1980s, a young British computer scientist named Tim Berners-Lee was working at CERN, the European research organization in Geneva, Switzerland. Scientists from all over the world were working together to try to solve some of the biggest mysteries of the universe. Berners-Lee wanted to come up with a way to make it easier for these scientists, who lived in many different countries, to communicate with each other and share their ideas.

Tim Berners-Lee, creator of the World Wide Web

Berners-Lee saw that the internet could be used to share all kinds of documents—what we now call web pages. Just like Gutenberg in the fifteenth century, Berners-Lee had to solve some tricky problems first. He had to figure out how to give every page on the internet a unique name or address. (We now call these Uniform Resource Locators, or URLs.) He had to design software that would allow people to browse web pages—software we now call browsers. He also had to create a computer language for making web pages, so they would look the same on all browsers. He solved those big problems—and countless small ones along the way—and invented what we now call the World Wide Web.

Before the web, just about the only people who used the internet were scientists and computer experts. After the web, anybody could publish whatever they wanted and put it out for anyone else to read or see. The revolution in communications technology begun by the invention of the web was easily as sweeping as the invention of the printing press. If anyone can be called a modern-day Gutenberg, it is Timothy Berners-Lee.

PROJECT GUTENBERG

Project Gutenberg is a volunteer effort to get public domain books digitized and online so that they will be available free for anyone to read. Being in the public domain means that the text of the book is no longer subject to copyright restrictions and thus belongs to everyone now. This covers many valuable classical and scholarly books and much great literature. Works by William Shakespeare and Jane Austen, Mary Shelley's *Frankenstein* and Mark Twain's *Adventures of Huckleberry Finn* are just a few books available at Project Gutenberg. As soon as new works move into the public domain, they are added to Project Gutenberg's collection.

The project was begun in 1971 by Michael Hart, the inventor of the electronic book. He was inspired by reading the US Declaration of Independence. He typed it into his computer and shared it with a few friends. Then he realized that any book could be shared this way, made available to anyone who wanted to read it for free. So far, there are around fifty thousand electronic books in the Project Gutenberg catalogue.

Disruptions

Inventions like the printing press and the World Wide Web are often said to be disruptive. They change the world in ways both small and large. These changes are usually unexpected. Gutenberg's printing press disrupted the dominance of the Catholic Church and made possible the Protestant Revolution, the Enlightenment, and democracy. It is difficult to overestimate how radically the world changed because of this invention. Today's changes in how information is created and shared are just as disruptive. In much the same way the printing press disrupted the dominance of the Catholic Church, web publishing disrupted the dominance of the print media.

From the days of the first newspapers, the press has been an important source of information for the reading public. In free nations, reporters and writers keep up with what the world's leaders are doing and make sure the public is informed. The system hasn't always worked smoothly, but it has served as an important check on power. Today, the explosion of web publishing is endangering that system. It is also providing new ways for the public to keep an eye on their leaders.

In the past, governments and militaries could easily deceive people about what they were up to. That is not so easy now. A citizen with a cell phone can film an instance of police injustice and post it on social media and other websites for everyone to see. Politicians once could get away with telling one group of voters one thing and another something quite different. That's much harder to do now that reports of previous statements can be searched quickly and easily online. The ease of publishing has given the average citizen the chance (and perhaps the responsibility) to call their leaders to account in ways that were once available only to the press.

Of course, the public can't do everything as well as the press. The more information is available, the greater the need for the press to serve as a reliable source of information for citizens. At the same time, the prevalence of online publishing has empowered the public, endangered the press, and exposed the vulnerabilities of free speech.

Newspapers and magazines can publish on the web just like anyone else. Publishing is practically free after you buy the computer and pay for internet access. Journalism, however, isn't free. To provide the kind of journalism that supports an open and democratic society, newspapers must hire writers and pay for travel and other costs of reporting. Having opinions about world events costs nothing. Finding out what is actually happening in the world is difficult, expensive, and often dangerous.

DID YOU KNOW:

Since the first blog was created in 1994, the number of blogs has grown to around thirty million in 2018.

Competing with free content on the web has made it difficult for newspapers and magazines to survive. That, in turn, has made it difficult for the public to stay informed.

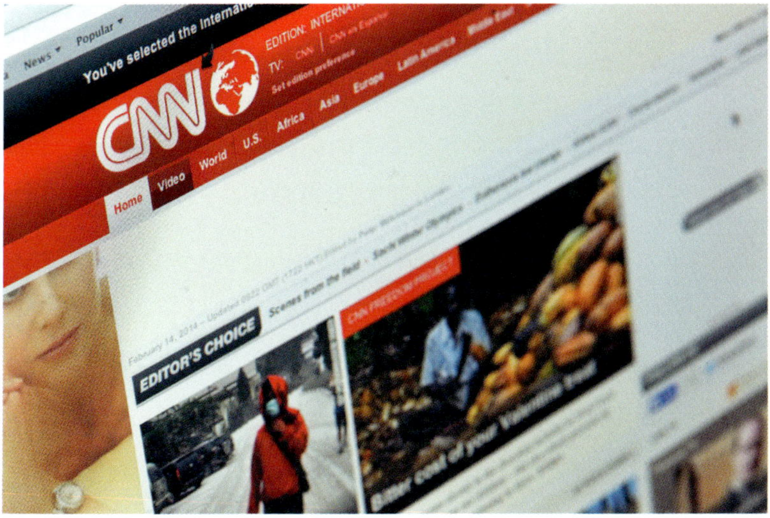

Major media outlets post articles on the web. However, much of the work of gathering and verifying that information still has to be done on the ground.

Many articles are published every day, but sometimes it can be hard to tell which ones are based on solid reporting and hard facts and which are made up. Those who want to weaken democracy take advantage of this problem by seeding the web with false and divisive information. Some people think the web could eventually mean the end of democratic governments.

However, history suggests otherwise. As literacy and access to books, newspapers, and other reading material has increased, so has the freedom and standard of living of the world's people. Problems still have to be sorted out, but there is reason to be optimistic that the changes that Gutenberg's machine brought to the world will continue to improve it.

GLOSSARY

calligrapher Someone who practices the art of decorative handwriting or lettering.

clergy Ordained members of a religion, for example priests and monks.

heresy Beliefs or statements that contradict the official position of a church or other religious organization.

journalism The field of news collecting, writing, and sharing via newspapers, magazines, and the web.

Linotype The trademarked name of a machine that produced type in single strips of metal.

literate Having the ability to read and write.

liturgy The official and formal readings of religious ceremonies.

manuscript The text of a book or other literary work before it is published.

medieval Relating to the Middle Ages, the period in Europe between about 500 and 1500 CE.

Mesoamerica The area from Mexico through Central America, home to many pre-Columbian civilizations.

plague A highly contagious and deadly bacterial infection that circulated periodically in medieval Europe, killing millions; bubonic plague.

primer A textbook used to teach basic subjects, such as reading and spelling.

public domain Information, such as books, that no longer has copyright restrictions and now belongs to the community, able to be used by anyone.

rotary press A printing press that prints by feeding paper between two rotating cylinders.

settlement An official agreement to end a lawsuit or other legal dispute.

theology The academic study of religious practices and beliefs.

thesis A position about an issue to be argued and debated; an argument or claim (the plural is theses).

type A piece of metal with a character cut into it, used for printing.

FURTHER INFORMATION

Books

Enzo, George. *The Reformation*. Primary Sources of World History. New York: Cavendish Square, 2017.

Rees, Fran. *Johannes Gutenberg: Inventor of the Printing Press*. Minneapolis MN: Compass Point, 2006.

Watson, Danielle. *The Church in Medieval Europe*. Life in Medieval Europe. New York: Cavendish Square, 2017.

Yomtov, Nel. *How the Printing Press Changed History*. Essential Library of Inventions. North Mankato, MN: ABDO Publishing, 2016.

Websites

Gutenberg Bible Exhibit at the Library of Congress

https://www.loc.gov/exhibits/bibles/the-gutenberg-bible.html

This website contains information and interactive images of the Library of Congress's copy of a Gutenberg Bible.

Project Gutenberg

http://www.gutenberg.org

This site provides a searchable database of free e-books in a variety of formats and languages, as well as details about the history and philosophy of Project Gutenberg.

Read, Write, Think

http://www.readwritethink.org/classroom-resources/student-interactives/printing-press-30036.html?tab=5#tabs

This site, aimed at students and teachers, offers an interactive game with templates students can use to create their own newspaper, magazine, or brochure.

Videos

Folger Library: Printing 101

https://www.youtube.com/watch?v=CN_KhB9SjVs

This site has a charming and informative demonstration of a Renaissance press, such as would have been used to print William Shakespeare's plays.

Getty Museum: The Structure of a Medieval Manuscript

https://www.youtube.com/watch?v=HKBJkf2xbqI

Visitors to this page learn how medieval manuscripts were made.

Teen Kids News: How a Gutenberg Printing Press Works

https://www.youtube.com/watch?v=kiD8U4gR0lA

In this video, a journalist from Teen Kid News visits a master printer to get a demonstration of a Gutenberg-style printing press.

SELECTED BIBLIOGRAPHY

Bernstein, William J. *Masters of the Word: How Media Shaped History from the Alphabet to the Internet*. New York: Grove Press, 2013.

Boissoneault, Lorraine. "A Brief History of Book Burning, from the Printing Press to Internet Archives." *Smithsonian*, August 31, 2017. https://www.smithsonianmag.com/history/brief-history-book-burning-printing-press-internet-archives-180964697.

Bovey, Alixe. "Church in the Middle Ages: From Dedication to Dissent." British Library, April 30, 2015. https://www.bl.uk/the-middle-ages/articles/church-in-the-middle-ages-from-dedication-to-dissent.

Cave, Roderick, and Sara Ayad. *The History of the Book in 100 Books: The Complete Story, from Egypt to E-Book*. Buffalo, NY: Firefly, 2012.

Cybulskie, Danièle. "Copycat: The Life of a Medieval Scribe." Medievalists.net, June 19, 2014. http://www.medievalists.net/2014/06/copycat-life-medieval-scribe.

Eisenstein, Elizabeth. *The Printing Revolution in Early Modern Europe*, 2nd ed. Cambridge, UK: Cambridge University Press, 2005.

Ferguson, Niall. *The Square and the Tower: Networks and Power, From the Freemasons to Facebook*. New York: Penguin, 2017.

Greenblatt, Stephen. *The Swerve: How the World Became Modern*. New York: W. W. Norton, 2011.

Houston, Keith. *The Book: A Cover-to-Cover Exploration of the Most Powerful Object of our Time*. New York: W. W. Norton, 2016.

Manguel, Alberto. *The Library at Night*. New Haven, CT: Yale University Press, 2006.

Naughton, John. *From Gutenberg to Zuckerberg: Disruptive Innovation in the Age of the Internet*. New York: Quercus, 2014.

Packer, George. "Cheap Words: Amazon Is Good for Customers, But Is It Good for Books?" *New Yorker*, February 17 and February 24, 2014.

Pettegree, Andrew. *Brand Luther: How an Unheralded Monk Turned His Small Town into a Center of Publishing, Made Himself the Most Famous Man in Europe—and Started the Protestant Reformation*. New York: Penguin, 2015.

Tarnoff, Ben. "How the Internet Was Invented." *Guardian*, July 15, 2016. https://www.theguardian.com/technology/2016/jul/15/how-the-internet-was-invented-1976-arpa-kahn-cerf.

INDEX

ABOUT THE AUTHOR

Avery Elizabeth Hurt is the author of many books for children and young adults, including a book on the code breakers and spies of the Cold War, a history of climate change science, and a biography of Ada Lovelace. She was working for her college newspaper when they first got desktop publishing—and she hasn't looked back.